Disney
WRECK-IT RALPH

Read-Along
STORYBOOK AND CD

Wreck-It Ralph is a video-game Bad Guy who wants to prove he can be a hero. To find out what happens, read along with me in your book. You will know it's time to turn the page when you hear this sound. . . . Let's begin now.

Play
Track 1
on your
CD now!

Movie Night

Printed in the United States of America

First Edition, October 2018   10 9 8 7 6 5 4 3 2 1

Library of Congress Control Number: 2018934260

ISBN 978-1-368-02864-6   FAC-038091-18236

For more Disney Press fun, visit www.disneybooks.com

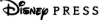
Disney PRESS
Los Angeles • New York

SUSTAINABLE FORESTRY INITIATIVE   Certified Sourcing
www.sfiprogram.org
SFI-00993
Logo Applies to Text Stock Only

Wreck-It Ralph was a Bad Guy. His job was to destroy things inside an arcade video game called Fix-It Felix, Jr.

As soon as the game started, Ralph began smashing buildings. "I'm gonna wreck it!"

Fix-It Felix was the hero of the game. He repaired everything that Ralph wrecked. "I can fix it!"

Every time a kid beat the game, Felix won a medal. Then the Nicelanders would yell at Ralph and throw him in the mud.

Ralph tried not to mind. After all, every game needed a Bad Guy.

One day, Ralph decided that he'd had enough. He snuck out of Fix-It Felix, Jr. and went into a video game called Hero's Duty. If Ralph got past all the evil cy-bugs and their eggs, he would win the Medal of Heroes.

Ralph was sure that would prove he was a Good Guy!
But just as Ralph grabbed the medal, a cy-bug attacked him!
They fell into an escape pod, and the ship's computer came online.

Ralph and the cy-bug launched across the arcade. They crashed into another game called Sugar Rush. Everything there was made out of candy.

Ralph was upset. "Oh, no. This is that candy go-kart game over by the whack-a-mole!" Ralph managed to get free from the escape pod. But the cy-bug sank into a sea of taffy.

Meanwhile, the Nicelanders in Fix-It Felix, Jr. were in big trouble. Without Ralph wrecking things, kids thought the game was broken. A giant OUT OF ORDER sign was put on it.

Felix set out to find Ralph. "It is my job to fix what Ralph wrecks."

Back in Sugar Rush, Ralph realized his medal was missing. It had landed in a tree when the pod crashed. He started climbing.

"You're not from here, are you?" A little girl named Vanellope von Schweetz was also in the tree. She noticed Ralph's medal. "Sweet mother of monkey milk, a gold coin!"

Vanellope snatched the medal away from Ralph. She hurried
to the other side of the kingdom. A kart race was about to begin.
King Candy was in charge. He explained the rules.
"The first nine racers across that finish line will represent
Sugar Rush as tomorrow's avatars."
The entry fee for the race was one gold coin.

Vanellope ran up and tossed Ralph's golden medal into the entry pot. The crowd gasped.

"The glitch!"

Vanellope wanted to race more than anything. But she wasn't supposed to. There was a problem with her programming. Everyone thought that the arcade would put Sugar Rush out of order if she competed.

Just then, Ralph showed up. He had fallen into a taffy pool and was covered in sticky candy.

He chased Vanellope. "You! Give me back my medal right now!"

Ralph finally caught up to Vanellope. By that point, he
was clean from the taffy. Just before he reached Vanellope, he
overheard the other racers in Sugar Rush teasing her.
They threw her in the mud and smashed her kart!
That made Ralph angry. "Hey! Leave her alone!"

He chased the kids away.

Afterward, Vanellope told Ralph she had a plan. "You help me get a new kart, a real kart, and I'll win the race and get you back your medal."

Ralph reluctantly agreed. "You better win."

Meanwhile, Felix had tracked Ralph to Sugar Rush. He joined forces with Sergeant Calhoun from Hero's Duty. Calhoun wanted to make sure no cy-bugs had escaped from her game. Felix wanted to bring Ralph home so he couldn't "go Turbo."

Felix explained that when the arcade had first opened, Turbo was the star of a popular game called Turbo Time.

But when a newer, fancier game came to the arcade, Turbo was jealous. He took it over, and kids thought it was broken. Turbo ended up putting both games and himself out of order, for good. Felix needed to bring Ralph home, or the same thing would happen to his game.

On the other side of the kingdom, Ralph and Vanellope were busy baking a kart. It was very complicated. In the end, the kart turned out lumpy. And it was covered in crazy decorations. Ralph thought it was a disaster.

But Vanellope was thrilled. She finally had a real racing kart! When Ralph saw her face, he couldn't help feeling a little proud.

It was almost time for the race. Vanellope ran to get something. Just then, King Candy showed up—with Ralph's medal.

He explained that Vanellope was never meant to be in Sugar Rush. If she raced, kids would think the game had glitches. It would go out of order, and Vanellope would disappear . . . forever.

"I know it's tough. But heroes have to make the tough choices, don't they? She can't race, Ralph." The king offered to give Ralph his medal back as long as he promised to keep Vanellope from racing.

Ralph reluctantly agreed. He wanted Vanellope to stay safe.

King Candy left just as Vanellope returned. She had made a special medallion for Ralph. It said, YOU'RE MY HERO.

Ralph felt terrible. He had to tell her the bad news. "Look, you can't be a racer."

Vanellope saw that Ralph had his medal back and thought he had turned against her. "You're a rat, and I don't need you, and I can win the race on my own."

Ralph realized there was only one way to keep Vanellope from racing. He smashed her kart.

"You really are a bad guy." Vanellope ran off in tears.

Ralph sadly headed back to the Fix-It Felix, Jr. game. When he got there, he noticed something strange. Across the arcade he could see the Sugar Rush game console. It showed pictures of all the racers. And Vanellope was one of them!

Vanellope wasn't a glitch. King Candy had lied to him!

Ralph realized that King Candy had messed with Vanellope's programming. If Vanellope crossed the race's finish line, the game would reset and her programming would be restored. Ralph dashed back to Sugar Rush.

He found Felix trapped in King Candy's dungeon. Ralph begged him to repair Vanellope's broken kart.

"There's a little girl whose only hope is this kart. Please, Felix, fix it, and I promise I will never try to be good again."

Felix fixed the kart in no time.
Together, the friends found Vanellope.
They needed to get her to the race.

By the time they reached the track, the competition had already begun. Vanellope caught up with the other karts lickety-split.

Soon she was neck and neck with King Candy.

The king was furious. He tried to run Vanellope off the track.
King Candy banged into her . . . and then he began to glitch.

He transformed into Turbo! The crowd screamed. King Candy was really Turbo!

Suddenly, the ground exploded! Hundreds of cy-bugs crawled out. Ralph realized they were going to destroy Sugar Rush.

Just then, he had an idea. Cy-bugs were attracted to bright things. Ralph climbed to the top of a tall mountain and wrecked it. A bright stream of diet soda shot out.

The cy-bugs flew straight into the geyser and were vaporized! A cy-bug chomped Turbo and flew into the soda, too.

Ralph was about to fall in. Suddenly, Vanellope zoomed up on her kart. She rescued Ralph from the mountain just in time.

They were both heroes!

Back at the finish line, Vanellope climbed into her kart. Ralph smiled. "You ready for this?"

Vanellope took a deep breath. "As ready as I'll ever be."

Ralph pushed her across the finish line. Then something incredible happened. Vanellope's programming was restored . . .

. . . and she transformed into a princess!
It turned out Vanellope wasn't just a racer.
She was the true leader of Sugar Rush.
Everyone cheered.

Ralph and Vanellope hugged good-bye. It was time for Ralph, Felix, and Calhoun to go home.

Back in Fix-It Felix, Jr., things were different for Ralph. The Nicelanders appreciated his wrecking, and they were much kinder to him. And Ralph decided that as long as he had Vanellope's friendship, he didn't need a medal to prove he was good, after all.

Because if a little girl like Vanellope liked him, how bad could he be?

Read-Along

STORYBOOK AND CD

Play **Track 2** on your CD now!

This is the story of two sisters named Anna and Elsa. You can read along with me in your book. You will know it is time to turn the page when you hear this sound. . . . Let's begin now.

Disney PRESS

Los Angeles • New York

When Princess Elsa and Princess Anna of Arendelle were little girls, they were the best of friends. Anna was one of the only people who knew Elsa's secret: Elsa had the power to make snow and ice with just her hands!

One night, Elsa filled an empty ballroom with snow. The sisters played together, building a snowman, sledding, and ice-skating.

But as they played, Elsa lost control. She accidentally hit Anna with a blast of icy magic! Anna was badly hurt, so her parents went to the ancient mountain trolls for help. There, a wise old troll told them that Anna could be saved—she was lucky to have been hit in the head, not the heart.

Even though Anna got better, her parents worried that
people would fear Elsa's powers. To keep her gift a secret, they
surrounded the castle with walls and never let anyone inside.

But whenever Elsa had strong feelings, the magic still
spilled out. Elsa didn't want to hurt her sister again, so she
never played with Anna. That made Anna feel very lonely.

Even after their parents were lost in a storm at sea, the
sisters didn't spend any time together.

Years later, it was time for Elsa to become queen of Arendelle. For just that day, the castle gates were opened! Hundreds of people attended the crowning ceremony. Elsa worked hard to hide her feelings—and her powers!

Anna loved meeting all the new people. "I wish it could be like this all the time."

"Me too."

At the coronation party, Anna danced with handsome Prince Hans from the Southern Isles. He made her heart flutter. It seemed like they had everything in common.

Because the gates were just open for one day, Hans and
Anna knew this was their only chance to be together. "Can
I say something crazy? Will you marry me?"
    "Yes!"

Anna and Hans asked Elsa for her blessing. But Elsa thought their engagement was a bad idea. "You can't marry a man you just met. My answer is no."

Anna couldn't believe it. "Why do you shut me out? What are you so afraid of?"

Elsa started to lose control. "Enough!" As she shouted, ice shot from her hands. Everyone stared at Elsa in shock. Now all of Arendelle knew Elsa's secret! Elsa panicked and fled for the mountains.

Anna felt horrible! Elsa's out-of-control powers had created
a terrible winter storm—in the middle of summer! "I'll bring
her back, and I'll make this right." She left Hans in charge of
the kingdom and raced after Elsa on her horse.

But as Anna rode through the fierce wind, her horse threw
her into the snow and ran off back to Arendelle.

Luckily, Anna met an ice harvester named Kristoff and his reindeer friend, Sven. She asked them for help. "I know how to stop this winter."

Together, they set off to look for Elsa.

As they climbed the mountain, Anna and Kristoff discovered a beautiful winter wonderland. There, they met an enchanted snowman named Olaf. Anna thought he looked familiar. "Olaf, did Elsa build you?"

Olaf smiled. "Yeah. Why?"

"Do you know where she is?"

"Yeah. Why?"

Kristoff got to the point. "We need Elsa to bring back summer."

Olaf was eager to help them. "Come on!"

Meanwhile, Hans was hard at work helping the people of Arendelle. But when Anna's horse came back to the castle without her, Hans knew he couldn't stay.

"Princess Anna is in trouble." Hans turned to the crowd. "I need volunteers to go with me to find her!" Soon Hans and some soldiers set out in search of Anna—and Elsa.

Back on the mountain, Olaf led Anna and Kristoff to a giant ice palace that Elsa had created with her powers.

Even Kristoff was impressed. "Now that's ice."

Inside, Anna told Elsa about the terrible storm in Arendelle. "It's okay. You can just unfreeze it."

Elsa looked worried. "I don't know how."

"That's not good."

Elsa was afraid that if she went back, she would just make the storm worse. Arendelle—and Anna—might be better off without her. "What am I going to do?"

Anna tried over and over again to convince Elsa to come home. But Elsa was too scared that she would hurt more people. As Elsa argued with her sister, an icy wave of magic burst from her body—and struck Anna in the chest! "Anna!"

Anna stood up and looked at Elsa. "No. I'm not leaving without you, Elsa."

"Yes, you are." Elsa knew what she had to do.

Elsa used her magic to create a huge snowman. He chased the friends out of the palace and toward a tall cliff.

Kristoff pulled out a rope to help them climb down.

"What if we fall?"

"There's twenty feet of fresh powder down there. It will be like landing on a pillow . . . hopefully."

They leaped over the edge and landed safely on the fluffy snow below. They had escaped from the snowman, but Anna had other things to worry about. . . .

Anna's hair was turning snowy white!

"It's because she struck you, isn't it?" Kristoff brought Anna to the trolls, hoping they could help. One troll told them that Elsa's icy magic had struck Anna's heart. If the magic was not reversed, Anna would soon be frozen solid. Only an act of true love could thaw a frozen heart.

Anna knew she loved Hans—maybe a kiss from him would work! As the friends hurried toward Arendelle, Anna began to shiver. Kristoff was especially worried about her. He was starting to care for Anna.

At that moment, Hans and his soldiers had arrived at the ice palace and attacked Elsa. As she defended herself, Elsa trapped one of her attackers behind icy spikes.

Hans cried out to her. "Queen Elsa! Don't be the monster they fear you are."

Elsa paused, but in her moment of doubt, she was knocked out. The attackers brought her back to Arendelle and threw her in the dungeon.

When Anna arrived in Arendelle, she said good-bye to Kristoff and Olaf. Then she raced to see Hans.

As soon as they were alone, Anna asked Hans to save her with a kiss. But Hans refused! Anna realized that he had only pretended to love her. He wanted to take over Arendelle by getting rid of Anna and Elsa! "All that's left now is to kill Elsa and bring back summer."

Hans left Anna alone and shivering. Luckily, Olaf found her and helped her warm up by the fire. But Anna was still getting weaker and weaker.

As Anna told him about Hans's evil plan, Olaf glanced out the window and saw Kristoff racing toward the castle. He realized that Kristoff loved Anna. "There's your act of true love right there!" It was Kristoff that Anna needed to kiss! With the last of her strength, Anna struggled outside.

Meanwhile, Elsa had escaped from the dungeon, but Hans was close behind her. "Elsa, you can't run from this." Hans told Elsa about her magic blast to Anna's heart. "I tried to save her, but it was too late."

Elsa collapsed in the snow and closed her eyes. Everything she had done to protect her sister had failed. And it was all her fault.

Nearby, Anna was hurrying toward Kristoff when she heard the clang of Hans's sword. She turned and saw her sister—Elsa was in danger!

Instead of saving herself and running to Kristoff, Anna leaped in front of her sister. "No!"

As Hans swung his sword, it shattered against Anna's frozen body. She had turned to solid ice.

Elsa clutched her sister. "Oh, Anna. No. Please, no!" Suddenly, Anna began to thaw! Her arms, warm again, reached around Elsa, and the two sisters hugged.

As Olaf watched them, he remembered what the wise old troll had said: "An act of true love will thaw a frozen heart." Anna's love for Elsa had saved both of them—and the kingdom.

Soon the two sisters were best friends again, and summer had returned to Arendelle. Elsa even made Olaf a little snow cloud to keep him from melting.

One day, Elsa had a surprise for Anna—the castle gates were wide open! "We are never closing them again."

The sisters smiled at each other. Now everything was the way it was supposed to be.

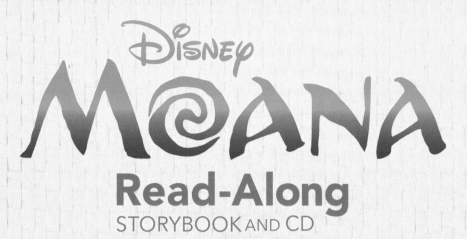

DISNEY
M⊚ANA
Read-Along
STORYBOOK AND CD

Play Track 3 on your CD now!

This is the story of Moana, the spirited daughter of a mighty chief, and Maui, the trickster demigod. You can read along with me in your book. You will know it is time to turn the page when you hear this sound. . . . Let's begin now.

DISNEP PRESS
Los Angeles • New York

"**In the beginning** there was only ocean—until an island emerged: the mother island, Te Fiti. Her heart had the power to create life itself. And she shared it with the world. But in time, some began to covet Te Fiti's heart. They thought if they possessed it, the power of creation would be theirs."

"And one day, the most brazen of them all voyaged across the vast ocean to take it. He was a demigod of the wind and sea. A shape-shifter, a trickster, a warrior who wielded a mighty magical fishhook. And his name was Maui."

In the village of Motunui, a group of small children gathered around Gramma Tala, listening to her tale.

"Without her heart, Te Fiti began to crumble, giving birth to a terrible darkness. Maui tried to escape but was confronted by another who sought the heart: Te Kā, a demon of earth and fire! Maui was struck from the sky, never to be seen again. And his magical fishhook and the heart of Te Fiti were lost to the sea."

Gramma Tala spoke of a terrible darkness spreading through the land. Her words frightened the children, and they burst into tears. But Moana, the chief's daughter, was not scared.

Gramma went on. "But one day, the heart will be found by someone who will journey beyond our reef, find Maui, deliver him across the great ocean to restore Te Fiti's heart, and save us all!"

Just then, Chief Tui appeared. Hearing the children's cries, he tried to comfort them. "No one ever needs to go outside our reef. We are safe. There is no darkness, there are no monsters."

　　While Chief Tui soothed the other children, young Moana slipped down to the beach. She was reaching for a beautiful shell at the edge of the water when she spied some large seabirds attacking a baby turtle. Moana hurried to help the turtle reach the water's edge.

　　Suddenly, the ocean waves beckoned Moana. Giggling, she stepped forward as the ocean played with her hair. Following the water away from the shore, Moana noticed a small stone with a strange spiral pattern on it. She had just grasped the object when her father called her name. *"Moana!"*

　　The ocean quickly whisked Moana back to the sandy shore. As she landed, the stone fell from her hand.

　　Tui picked up Moana. "Oh, yes, you are the next great chief of our people. And you will do wondrous things."

　　Moana took her father's hand and they turned toward the village. Behind them, unseen, Gramma Tala quietly plucked the half-buried stone from the sand.

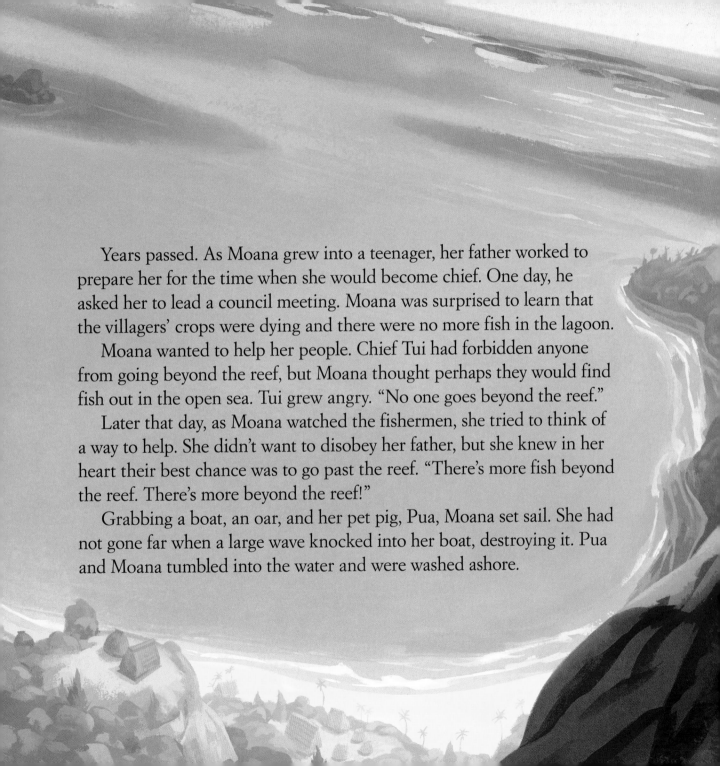

Years passed. As Moana grew into a teenager, her father worked to prepare her for the time when she would become chief. One day, he asked her to lead a council meeting. Moana was surprised to learn that the villagers' crops were dying and there were no more fish in the lagoon.

Moana wanted to help her people. Chief Tui had forbidden anyone from going beyond the reef, but Moana thought perhaps they would find fish out in the open sea. Tui grew angry. "No one goes beyond the reef."

Later that day, as Moana watched the fishermen, she tried to think of a way to help. She didn't want to disobey her father, but she knew in her heart their best chance was to go past the reef. "There's more fish beyond the reef. There's more beyond the reef!"

Grabbing a boat, an oar, and her pet pig, Pua, Moana set sail. She had not gone far when a large wave knocked into her boat, destroying it. Pua and Moana tumbled into the water and were washed ashore.

As Moana lay in the sand, discouraged, Gramma Tala appeared. Moana told her that her father was right. It seemed she wasn't meant to venture beyond the reef.

With a mysterious smile, Gramma Tala led Moana to a hidden cave. Moana was confused. "What's in there?"

Gramma handed Moana a torch. "The answer to the question you keep asking yourself: who are you meant to be? Go inside. Bang the drum and find out."

Moana entered the cavern. She could hardly believe her eyes. It was full of beautiful ancient boats! Moana climbed into the largest boat in the cavern. A log drum sat on the deck. Curious, she hit the drum.

The boats' sails seemed to come to life! Moana could feel her ancestors crossing the sea in search of new lands. Moana was amazed at the incredible discovery. "We were voyagers! Why'd we stop?"

Gramma Tala explained that the ships had stopped coming back when Maui stole the heart of Te Fiti. To protect their people, the ancient chiefs had forbidden any more voyages. But now the darkness that Maui had awakened had begun to spread across their island.

Gramma Tala gently pressed the heart of Te Fiti into Moana's hand. It was the stone the ocean had given Moana all those years before. Gramma Tala smiled. "The ocean chose you."

Moana had to do something! After racing back to the village, she burst into a council meeting. "We can save our island! We were voyagers; we can voyage again!"

Chief Tui was mad. He wished Moana would forget about the ocean.

Just then, a messenger brought terrible news. Gramma Tala was ill.

Moana hurried to her side. Gramma Tala urged her granddaughter to find Maui. "Follow the fishhook. And when you find Maui, you grab him by the ear and you say, 'I am Moana of Motunui. You will board my boat, sail across the sea, and restore the heart of Te Fiti.' Go."

Moana knew Gramma Tala was right. She took a boat from the cave and boldly set sail! At dawn, Moana discovered a stowaway. It was Heihei the rooster! When Heihei saw the water, he panicked.

Moana laughed. "The ocean is a friend of mine."

That night, a violent storm hit. Rocked by the waves, Moana's boat crashed on an island!

Moana and Heihei had landed on Maui's island. Moana tried to give her speech, but Maui cut her off. He was not interested in Moana. He was focused on something else. "Boat! A boat!"

Moana tried to tell Maui that he must go with her. "I'm here because you stole the heart of Te Fiti, and you will board my boat and sail across the sea and put it back."

But Maui would not listen. Instead, he used his tattoos to show Moana his great achievements—like bringing fire to mortals, lassoing the sun to make days longer, and even creating coconuts!

Maui wanted to leave the island. He trapped Moana in a cave and set sail in her boat. Moana escaped and swam toward Maui, but she couldn't catch up with him. Suddenly, the ocean lifted her onto the boat. Maui was stunned. "Did not see that coming."

The demigod tossed Moana into the water, but the ocean kept returning her to the boat. Moana held up the heart of Te Fiti. "I am Moana of Motunui and you will restore the heart!"

Maui backed away. "That is not a heart, it is a curse. If you don't put it away, bad things are going to come for it."

Just then, a huge spear slammed into the boat!

Maui looked around. "Kakamora. Murdering little pirates."

Suddenly, a group of small feisty warriors wearing coconut armor boarded the boat. In the confusion, the heart of Te Fiti fell from Moana's necklace and Heihei ate it! One of the Kakamora picked up Heihei.

Grabbing her oar, Moana raced after him. She knocked pirate after pirate out of her way. Finally, she whacked the thief over the head and took back Heihei, who coughed up the heart. Quickly, Moana and Maui raced away.

Moana knew that she needed Maui's help to reach Te Fiti and restore the heart. But Maui needed her help, too! Without his hook, he had no magic. Moana offered him a trade. "We get your hook, take out Te Kā, restore the heart. Deal?"

The demigod agreed. "Deal."

But getting the fishhook wouldn't be easy. It was being held by Tamatoa, a giant crab who collected shiny objects. Tamatoa lived in Lalotai—the realm of monsters. Maui and Moana climbed up a tall jagged rock and then jumped down . . . down . . . down . . . through a portal in the ocean to Lalotai.

Moana rushed into Tamatoa's cave, only to be captured by the monster. To her surprise, Maui came to her rescue and grabbed his hook. But when he tried to shape-shift and fly away, he couldn't. His hook wasn't working correctly!

As Tamatoa closed in on Maui, Moana held up the heart of Te Fiti. Then she dropped it to the ground. When Tamatoa lunged for it, Moana grabbed the fishhook. Tamatoa thought he got the heart, but Moana had tricked him. Tamatoa was left with a rock. Moana still had the heart!

Moana had kept her part of the deal. Now it was Maui's turn. Maui taught Moana how to sail and navigate by the stars. In return, Moana helped Maui relearn how to use his hook. The two began to earn each other's respect. As they approached the island of Te Fiti, smoke billowed into the sky. It was Te Kā, the lava monster. With Moana's encouragement, Maui felt confident that he could defeat Te Kā. "It's Maui time!"

The demigod transformed into a hawk and flew toward the blackened barrier islands around Te Fiti. Suddenly, Te Kā rose up and knocked Maui out of the sky!

Moana caught Maui in her boat. Maui told Moana to turn around; they weren't ready to face Te Kā. But Moana kept going. Te Kā brought its giant fist down toward their boat. At the last second, Maui raised his fishhook and blocked the blow! The impact created a tidal wave that carried Moana and Maui out into the ocean, far from Te Fiti.

Looking at Te Kā, Moana realized something. The monster was made of hot lava. It could not touch the cool ocean water. If Moana could distract Te Kā, maybe she could sneak past it.

Moana turned to Maui for help, but he refused. His fishhook had been damaged by Te Kā's blow. One more hit and it would be destroyed. "Without my hook, I am nothing. Good-bye, Moana."

Moana didn't know what to do. She needed Maui to restore the heart of Te Fiti. Holding up the heart, she showed it to Maui. "The ocean chose me."

But Maui just shook his head. "It chose wrong."

With that, Maui changed back into a hawk and flew away.

All alone, Moana dropped the heart of Te Fiti back into the ocean. "You have to choose someone else. Choose someone else."

Moana watched sadly as the heart sank. She had thought the ocean would tell her not to give up, but it was letting Moana make her own decision. Suddenly, a glowing manta ray rushed through the water toward her. A voice came from the bow of the boat. "You're a long ways past the reef."

It was Gramma Tala! She told Moana that she had been wrong to pressure her. "I never should have put so much on your shoulders. If you are ready to go home, I will be with you."

Moana nodded and put her oar in the water. Then she hesitated. She no longer knew what was the right thing to do. Listening, she tried to find her inner voice again. Finally, the answer came to her. She was Moana. She loved her people and the sea. She was a wayfinder.

Moana dove into the dark water. Far below on the ocean floor, the heart of Te Fiti began to glow. After what felt like forever, Moana's fingers closed around the heart. When she resurfaced, Gramma Tala was gone, but Moana knew her grandmother was always with her.

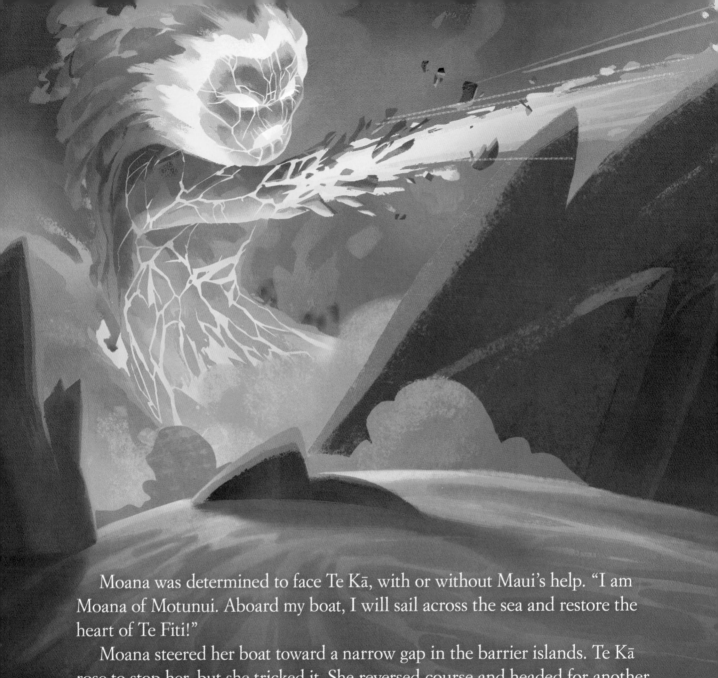

Moana was determined to face Te Kā, with or without Maui's help. "I am
Moana of Motunui. Aboard my boat, I will sail across the sea and restore the
heart of Te Fiti!"

Moana steered her boat toward a narrow gap in the barrier islands. Te Kā
rose to stop her, but she tricked it. She reversed course and headed for another
opening. Te Kā hurled boulders at her, but Moana made it through! "We did it!"

Moana looked around. "Heihei!" Heihei had fallen overboard!

When Moana turned around to save the rooster, Te Kā tipped over the boat. Then, raising its fist, Te Kā prepared to smash the vessel to bits.

At that second, Maui returned to help Moana! He had realized that he didn't need the fishhook to be himself. The demigod blocked Te Kā's blow with his cracked fishhook. "I've got your back, Chosen One. Go save the world!"

Moana and Heihei climbed back into the boat. "Wait, Maui. Thank you." He grinned. "You're welcome!"

With Maui holding Te Kā at bay, Moana reached Te Fiti. She raced up a slope and stopped short. Where Te Fiti should have been was an empty crater!

Maui flew toward the lava monster, but Te Kā knocked him to the ground, shattering his hook!

As Moana stared at Te Kā, she caught a glimpse of a familiar spiral in its chest. Suddenly, Moana knew exactly what to do. She held up the heart, instructing the water to let her through. The water pulled away from the shore, clearing a path for the angry Te Kā to reach Moana.

The monster raced toward her, but Moana stood tall, unafraid. Then a low sweet song filled the air. Te Kā grew calm. As the monster reached her, Moana touched her forehead to Te Kā's and told it to remember who it was.

At that, Te Kā's rocky exterior fell away. Inside was a kind, smiling face. It was Te Fiti! Her life-giving heart had been returned, transforming her back into her true self. A crown of flowers blossomed on Te Fiti's head!

Te Fiti thanked Moana and Maui. She repaired Moana's canoe and restored Maui's shattered fishhook.

As Maui prepared to leave, Moana had a suggestion. "You could come with us, you know. My people are going to need a master wayfinder."

Maui gave Moana a hug. "They already have one."

A new tattoo appeared over Maui's heart. It was Moana the wayfinder. Maui turned into a hawk once more and flew off.

Moana set a course for home. Behind her, the green island of Te Fiti bloomed. On Motunui, Moana's mother and father noticed the land turning green again. Together, they raced down to the water's edge. They knew that Moana would return, triumphant. A moment later, the shadow of Moana's boat emerged from the horizon line. The great wayfinder was home.

With Te Fiti restored, everything on Motunui began to bloom again. The villagers pulled the ancient boats from the cave and repaired them. The time for voyaging had returned. It was time for the people of Motunui to remember who they were. It was time for Moana to lead her people on new adventures across the sea!